This is a story about Rinkle-Ronkle the
Rhinocerwurst. A Rhinocerwurst is a first cousin
to the Rhinoceros.

 Parents will be delighted with Rinkle-Ronkle, and
so will children of all ages. Rinkle-Ronkle is big and
strong, but also very gentle. He loves children and
always looks out for them, to keep them from harm
and from wrong. Rinkle-Ronkle has a big, kind
heart. He can talk, too!

 He is also very funny, and makes children laugh--
and he makes their parents laugh, too!

 So, come along and get acquainted with one of the
most delightful animals you'll ever meet--
Rinkle-Ronkle the Rhinocerwurst!

RINKLE-RONKLE

THE RHINOCERWURST

™

For Connie, my beloved wife

and for our dear children and their spouses:
Lynn, Mark and Shelley, Dan and Robyn, Beth and John

and for our precious grandchildren:
Erin, Chelsea, Gabi, Joshua, Abby, and Rylea

Printed in the United States of America.

Library of Congress Catalog Card Number: 97-94220
ISBN: 0-9659681-0-3

RINKLE-RONKLE
THE
RHINOCERWURST

AND THE BIG
CHOCOLATE MILK SPILL

BY DR. PAUL

Published by FDI Group
Cordova, Tennessee

It was a beautiful day. Rinkle-Ronkle the Rhinocerwurst was playing with Erin, Chelsea, Baby Rylea, Gabi, Joshua, and Abby in Granddaddy and Grandmother's yard.

Rinkle-Ronkle loves children. He also likes to smell the nice flowers. Granddaddy and Grandmother are always glad for Rinkle-Ronkle to visit.

Erin said, "Today I helped my Mom fold clothes.
I like being a helper."

Chelsea said, "I helped my Mother wash dishes
today. It's fun to get my hands in the soap suds and
help my Mother!"

Abby said, "I helped my Daddy make pancakes this morning. M-m-m-m-m GOOD!"

Gabi said, "I helped Mother sweep the kitchen. It felt nice to be a helper."

Joshua said, "I helped my Daddy pick up leaves today. It's COOL to be a helper!"

Baby Rylea said, "GNXPLZRL!" (She meant, "Today I helped my Daddy color pictures. I like to help Daddy color.")

Rinkle-Ronkle said, "I like to be a helper, too.
What can I do to help someone today?"

Erin replied, "I don't know, Rinkle-Ronkle. But just you wait, you'll think of something. You always do."

Then they all heard a loud "TOOT! TOOT!" It was the train. They stopped playing so they could watch it go by.

"Look," said Erin. "It's a train load of chocolate milk from the chocolate milk factory."

But all of a sudden something went wrong. One of the wheels came off the engine, and the whole train turned over.

Thankfully, no one was hurt, but chocolate milk began spilling everywhere!

It covered the streets. It covered people's yards. Chocolate milk ran everywhere!

Some of the folks climbed trees to keep from getting soaked with chocolate milk.

Other people got in boats and floated in the chocolate milk.

Everyone wanted to get rid of the chocolate milk, but no one knew how.

Then Rinkle-Ronkle said, "I will help!"

"But, Rinkle-Ronkle," said one of the men, "how can you help? You're a big, strong Rhinocerwurst, and we all love you. But how can you get rid of all this chocolate milk?"

Rinkle-Ronkle answered, "I'll show you if someone will get me a piece of garden hose."

Erin found an old piece of garden hose in Granddaddy's garage and brought it to Rinkle-Ronkle. "Here you are," she said.

Rinkle-Ronkle said, "Thank you. This will be
my soda straw. Watch!" Then he started drinking
up the chocolate milk through his straw.

He drank the chocolate milk out of people's yards.

He drank the chocolate milk out of the streets.

He drank the chocolate milk out of the ditches.

Soon all the chocolate milk was gone, and everyone was glad.

The Mayor of the town called for a big celebration.
All the people gathered to say "Thank you" to
Rinkle-Ronkle."

"Rinkle-Ronkle," said the Mayor, "you're our hero. What can we do to reward you?"

Rinkle-Ronkle said, "Can I have some more chocolate milk?"

"Yes!" answered the Mayor. "Bring our friend
Rinkle-Ronkle a big glass of chocolate milk!"
The Mayor's helper brought the chocolate milk.

So, Rinkle-Ronkle drank his chocolate milk.

SLURP!

When Rinkle-Ronkle finished his chocolate milk he said, "Thank you." Then he burped and said, "Oops! Excuse me, please!"

The Mayor said, "Rinkle-Ronkle, you're a great helper! Not everyone can drink up a big chocolate milk spill like you did, but everyone can find SOME way to be a helper!"

Then Rinkle-Ronkle and all six children went back to Granddaddy and Grandmother's yard to play.

The ground was still a little bit soggy, but they didn't mind. They were all happy, because every one of them--including Rinkle-Ronkle--had been a helper!

The End

To purchase additional copies of this book,
write to:

FDI Group
P.O. Box 1643
Cordova, TN 38088

Or call toll-free 1-888-4-RINKLE
(1-888-474-6553)